FRANKIE VS. THE COWBOY'S CREW

ALSO BY FRANK LAMPARD

Frankie vs. the Pirate Pillagers

Frankie vs. the Rowdy Romans

Frankie vs. the Cowboy's Crew

Frankie vs. the Mummy's Menace

FRANKIE VS. THE COWBOY'S CREW

FRANK LAMPARD

SCHOLASTIC INC.

ISBN 978-0-545-66616-9

Published by Scholastic Inc., 557 Broadway, New York, NY 10012, by arrangement with Little, Brown Books for Young Readers. SCHOLASTIC and associated logos are trademarks and/or registered trademarks of Scholastic Inc.

12 11 10 9 8 7 6 5 4 3 2 14 15 16 17 18 19/0

Printed in the U.S.A. 40
First printing, July 2014

To my mom, Pat,
who encouraged me to do my
homework in between kicking a ball
all around the house, and is still
with me every step of the way

Welcome to a fantastic fantasy league — the greatest soccer competition ever held in this world or any other!

You'll need four on a team, so choose carefully. This is a lot more serious than a game in the park. You'll never know who your next opponents will be, or where you'll face them.

So lace up your cleats, players, and good luck! The whistle's about to blow!

The Ref

CHAPTER 1

At the edge of the field, Max strained at his leash, barking loudly. Frankie knew how he felt. This game was *really* close. St. Peter's School had a good team. Maybe even as good as Frankie's. The score remained zero–zero, so the pressure was building. Lots of parents, including

Frankie's, had come out to watch the game.

"Concentrate, team!" called Mr. Donald, their soccer coach. "Two minutes to go! Play to the final whistle."

Charlie had the ball in his gloves in the center of the goal, looking for someone to throw it to. He saw Frankie's friend Kobe and rolled it out to him.

"Pass it, Kobe!" called Louise.

Kobe neatly sidestepped with the ball as one of the St. Peter's players ran toward him. He kicked a looping pass to Louise. She managed to cushion the ball on her knee.

"Great!" said a voice from the side of the field. "Pass it to a *girl*."

Frankie shot a frown at his brother, Kevin, who was holding Max's leash. "She's better than you, any day of the week," he shouted back.

Kevin made a face. "Whatever."

"Hit me, Louise!" yelled Frankie.

Louise looked up. Two opponents rushed at her. She stabbed the ball with her toe, and it sailed perfectly between them to Frankie's foot.

"Go on, son!" shouted his dad.

Frankie turned and ran toward the goal. It was just him and the goalie, a giant kid who'd stopped every shot so far.

"Shoot, Frankie!" yelled Louise.

The goalie started moving out from the goal, spreading his arms wide.

"You can do it!" called Frankie's mom.

Frankie wondered what to do. Dribble the ball around the goalie, or try for the chip over his head? The boy seemed taller by the second. He'd have to go around him. No problem. Frankie stepped over the ball, and dropped his shoulder to go left. The goalie kept his eyes on the ball. Frankie darted right. He was through . . .

Argh!

He felt his legs snag as the goalie stuck out a foot and tackled him. Frankie fell headlong onto the ground.

The crowd let out a groan.

Frankie sat up, a bit dizzy. The St. Peter's goalkeeper had the ball in his hands.

"Too bad," he said with a grin, then hurled the ball forward.

"Get up, Frankie!" yelled Mr. Donald.

Frankie scrambled to his feet and ran after it, but he was too far back. It felt like he was watching in slow motion. The opposition passed the ball expertly between themselves, avoiding Louise and Kobe and Matt. Their striker blasted the ball past Charlie and it nestled in the back of the goal.

The St. Peter's players piled on top of one another as the whistle blew.

One–nothing.

Frankie's team had lost!

They shook hands with the St. Peter's kids. Frankie couldn't look Louise in the eye.

"I don't know what happened," he said, feeling his face grow hot. "I messed up."

His friend patted him on the back. "Don't worry," she said. "We can't win every game."

As the teams left the field, Frankie's brother blocked his path. "Nice job, loser," he said.

"Leave him alone," said Charlie.

"Even *she* could have scored that," said Kevin, nodding at Louise.

"Is everything okay here?" asked Mr. Donald, glaring at Kevin.

"Just giving some encouragement, coach," sneered Kevin. Frankie's brother stalked off, tugging a whining Max with him.

Frankie sat on the grass and took off his cleats. As he dropped them into his bag, his battered soccer ball rolled out.

"Oh no," said Mr. Donald. "If you've been practicing with that old thing, it's no surprise you've been struggling."

Frankie shared a glance with Charlie and Louise. True, the ball *did* look like it had been chewed up and spit out, but only Frankie and his friends knew that the ball's appearance was deceiving. The soccer ball was magic — a gateway to other worlds. He couldn't help the flicker of a smile on his lips.

"I don't think it's funny," said Mr. Donald. "You shouldn't try so many tricks, Frankie. Just get the basics right."

"Sorry, coach, it's just . . ." Frankie began.

But Mr. Donald had walked away.

Frankie's dad came over with Max. "You want a ride home, Frankie?" he asked. "We have to go shopping to get Kevin some new clothes."

Frankie shook his head. He couldn't think of anything worse than sharing the backseat with his older brother taunting him. "It's okay, Dad," he said. "I'll walk Max back. We'll go the long way, through the fields."

"We'll come with you," said Louise.

"Yeah, we can get a snack on the way!" said Charlie.

They didn't talk about the game on the way home, which suited Frankie fine. It wasn't like him to lose his nerve at all. He kept replaying the missed shot in his head, wondering what he could have done differently.

Their route back to town took them past Evans Farm.

"I'll show you the horses," said Louise.

Louise mucked out the stables at the farm every weekend, and in return was allowed to ride some of the horses. The farmer, Mr. Evans, was fixing a fence post near the road.

"Hello, Louise!" he said, waving a mallet.

"Hi, Mr. Evans," said Louise. "Do you mind if I take my friends to see Tinkerbelle?"

"Go right ahead," said the farmer.

"*Tinkerbelle?*" said Charlie as they crossed the yard. "What a silly name for a horse!"

Louise led them into a barn, past rows of empty stalls. As they reached the last stall, Louise said, "Meet Tinkerbelle."

Charlie gasped and took a step

back as a huge black head peered over the door. "He's a giant!" he said.

Louise grinned. "He's a she, actually. Sixteen and a half hands tall. Big softy, though, aren't you?" she said, stroking the horse's nose.

Max gave a little bark, and Tinkerbelle tossed her mane.

"Do you want to say hello, Frankie?" Louise asked.

Frankie let the soccer ball roll out of his bag. "That's okay," he said glumly. He practiced a couple of step overs. Maybe Mr. Donald was right. He'd tried to be too fancy.

Charlie slowly approached Tinker-belle, his gloved hand outstretched.

"Why don't you take those off?" asked Louise. "She won't bite."

Charlie chuckled. "No way. You know me — always ready."

Frankie managed a smile. He spotted a horseshoe hanging on a nail on the wall opposite the stall.

They were supposed to be good luck, weren't they?

Maybe if I can hit the horseshoe with the ball, I'll get lucky in front of the goal next time, he thought.

He took aim, then gently chipped the ball. It sailed in a perfect arc toward the horseshoe . . .

. . . and vanished.

"Um . . . guys," he said, turning toward his friends.

Tinkerbelle gave a panicked snort, and Louise and Charlie spun around.

"Uh-oh," said Charlie.

"Cool!" said Louise.

Max yelped.

The horseshoe and the stable wall were gone, replaced with a swirl of color.

"Ready for another adventure?" asked Frankie.

CHAPTER 2

Frankie led the way, closing his eyes as he passed through the wall. When he opened them, the farm was gone. He found himself standing at the end of a dusty street lined with ramshackle wooden buildings. One had a "General Store" sign above the door. Another looked like a saloon, with a wooden porch and swing doors. Shutters covered most of the windows. Beyond the street stretched miles of sandy desert dotted with cacti, and in the distance mountains rose in a haze of heat. What looked like a single line of railroad track vanished into the distance. The magic soccer ball was resting alongside a water trough outside a blacksmith's stall.

Frankie sniffed — the air smelled strangely sweet, like caramel.

"Where *are* we?" asked Charlie. Instead of his uniform, he was now wearing faded jeans and shirt with a neckerchief and a wide-brimmed hat.

"*When* are we?" asked Louise, who was tugging at the hem of a fancy red dress. "This is not my style at all!"

Frankie glanced down at his own clothes. He saw boots with spurs, pants with leather chaps, and a brown shirt. Stitched onto the shirt was his FFC logo.

We must be here to play a game!

Max scampered along, sniffing the ground. "Looks like the Wild West to me!" he barked.

"How do you know?" asked Frankie.

The little dog wagged his tail. "You know when your dad's asleep on the sofa on Sunday afternoons with the TV on?"

"Yes," said Frankie.

"Well, I watch the Westerns," said Max. "I love John Wayne. Plus, you're wearing a cowboy hat. It's really obvious."

Frankie reached up and felt the hat on his head. "Oh, yeah."

"Let's explore," said Louise.

As they walked slowly up the middle of the street, eerie silence settled over them. Gusts of wind blew in from time to time, scattering sand in the air.

"Where are all the people?" asked Charlie, shielding his eyes from the glaring sun. "This place seems deserted."

Frankie thought he saw the shape of a face in a window, but it quickly vanished.

"They are all hiding," he said. *I wonder why.*

But not everyone was indoors. A grand white building stood at the end of the street. Above the double doors, a man with a rag stood at the top of a ladder. He was polishing a large clock that said it was eleven o'clock.

As they approached, Frankie spied a sign hanging above the doors that read EXPRESS TRAIN COMING THROUGH AT TWELVE O'CLOCK TODAY!

"Hello there!" said Frankie.

The man spun around, and the ladder wobbled beneath him. Frankie rushed forward and grabbed it before it fell. The man wore a black suit with a thin black tie. A whistle hung around his neck. Beneath his bushy white beard, his face looked sort of familiar.

"You're the Ref!" said Frankie.

The man took out a pair of glasses from his top pocket and put them on.

He squinted at Frankie and his friends.

"I don't know what you're talking about," he said. "I'm the station-master here in Sweetsville."

"Sweetsville?" said Charlie. "Sounds like my kind of place!"

"We're Frankie's FC," said Louise.

The stationmaster climbed down from his ladder, then pointed to the clock. "You're early, then," he said.

"Early for what?" barked Max.

The stationmaster didn't seem surprised that a dog was talking to him. He shambled inside the station building and came out clutching a newspaper. He opened it up so Frankie could read the front cover:

The Cowboy's Crew

vs.

Frankie's FC

The Sweetsville Showdown

High Noon!

"High noon!" said Charlie. "Cool!"

"That's twelve o'clock to you," said Max.

Charlie scowled. "I know that, fur-face."

Louise nudged Frankie. "I don't like the sound of the Cowboy's Crew," she said.

"No one does," said the station-master. "They are the meanest group of bandits this side of the mountains. Over in Candytown, they stole every bar of chocolate from the store. The kids there haven't seen anything sweet all summer!"

"That's awful!" said Charlie.

"And over by Jelly Mountain," said the stationmaster, "they blew up the sugar mines! The folks up there have to make cakes with salt instead of sugar!"

"Yuck!" said Louise.

So that's why everyone's hiding, thought Frankie.

"No point standing around here," said the stationmaster. "Why don't you go and rest in the saloon?" He nodded across the street. "No milkshakes, I'm afraid. The Cowboy's Crew made sure of that. Just water."

"A rest sounds good," said Charlie, fanning his hat in front of his face. "It's hot out here!"

"A glass of water will be fine," said Frankie, "but then we have to practice."

He led his team back across the street, kicking the ball in front of him. The Cowboy's Crew would be tough opponents, no doubt. *We'll have to do some passing drills. Then shooting.* A bead of sweat trickled down his back. *We'd better not tire ourselves out, though.*

Max ran ahead. "Let me go first, guys," he said. "In the movies, these saloons are a little rough-and-tumble. They don't like strangers, so you need to speak the lingo to fit in."

He scampered beneath the swing doors, and Frankie pushed through after him. A bell rang above.

"Howdy, partners," Max said. "We're just passin' by . . . Oh."

Frankie laughed. The saloon wasn't what he was expecting at all. There were no tables, no outlaws,

and no bar. In fact, it wasn't a saloon at all.

"Awesome!" said Charlie. "A candy store!"

But then his face fell, and Frankie saw why. Though hundreds of jars filled the shelves on the wall, nearly all were empty. Some had a few hard candies on the bottom, others contained one or two chocolates or toffees. Trays on the counter had a few dusty gumdrops. Frankie saw a pot with a single lollipop, and some ancient-looking jawbreakers and marshmallows.

"Coming!" called a voice, then a plump woman with frizzy hair shuffled up behind the counter. "Greetings," she said. "What can I . . . ?"

The shopkeeper trailed off and her face drained of color. She was staring at Louise and her mouth opened and closed like a gasping fish.

"Oh my giddy gumdrops!" she cried. Then she bustled out into the street screaming, "Sheriff! Sheriff Quigley! Come quick!"

CHAPTER 3

"What got into her?" asked Louise.

Charlie opened a jar on the counter and sniffed suspiciously. "Who knows?" he said. "Maybe she didn't like your dress!"

Frankie took the chocolate out of Charlie's hand and placed it on the counter. "These aren't ours," he said.

"Plus, we're playing in an hour. You don't want to get sick."

"She just walked in, plain as day!" came the shopkeeper's voice from outside. "Be careful, Sheriff. She's dangerous!"

The swing doors opened again, and a tall, gray-haired man wearing a starred sheriff's badge strode into the candy store. He placed his hands on his hips, and Frankie saw he had a gun in his holster. The woman who owned the store peered out from behind him, trembling.

"Listen here," he said. "We don't want any trouble, miss. You're coming with me to jail."

"Jail?" said Louise. "But I haven't done anything wrong."

"Don't make this hard," said the sheriff, stepping forward.

Charlie stood in his path, shielding Louise with his gloves. "You leave her alone!" he said.

Quick as a flash, the sheriff drew his six-shooter and fired at Charlie's feet. Max leapt into the air and Frankie froze.

When the smoke from the barrel cleared, Frankie saw something white smeared just in front of Charlie's toes. Max sniffed at it.

"Chewing gum," he growled.

"Ugh!" said Louise. "That's gross!"

"The next time you won't be so lucky," said the sheriff. "Out of the way, kid."

Charlie stood his ground, but Louise touched him on the shoulder. "It's all right," she said. "I'll go with him and get this sorted out."

The sheriff tied Louise's hands with what looked like a strawberry licorice and led her out of the shop. Frankie followed with Charlie and Max. The station clock read twenty past eleven. *We can't afford for Louise to be locked up,* he thought. *The game's in forty minutes, and we don't have any subs!*

"This is a big mistake," Max said.

"It was a mistake trying to rob my shop!" cried the shopkeeper. "I can't believe the legendary Miss Sue-Ann just rode into town."

"Who's Miss Sue-Ann?" asked Charlie.

The jailhouse was a stone building across the street from the saloon. Pinned to the front wall were several sheets of windblown paper, each one showing a drawing of a face with the word "WANTED" above. The sheriff pointed to one in the middle. "There she is!"

Frankie peered closer. The picture was of Louise! True, she had a bandana pulled up over her face,

WANTED
Miss Sue-Ann
Wanted for candy-rustling
Runs with the Cowboy's Crew,
the most fearsome gang in the Wild West!

but the eyes were the same and so was the hair. Beneath the portrait were the words: MISS SUE-ANN. WANTED FOR CANDY-RUSTLING. RUNS WITH THE COWBOY'S CREW, THE MOST FEARSOME GANG IN THE WILD WEST!

The sheriff opened the door. "Sandy!" he shouted. "You'll never guess who just moseyed on into town!" No answer came from inside. "Sandy?" Still nothing. Sheriff Quigley growled. "That good-fer-nothing . . ." he said. "Late again."

He unfastened Louise's wrists, shoved her inside, and then started munching on the strawberry licorice. He pointed a finger at Frankie's chest. "You and your sweet-toothed gang better lie low. Tex and the rest of the Cowboy's Crew will be here soon, and you don't want to get in their way."

"But we're here to play them!" said Frankie.

"Then good luck to you," said the sheriff. "You'll sure need it!"

He turned and followed Louise into the jailhouse, slamming the door behind him.

Charlie slumped onto the step and let his head fall into his gloves. "What do we do now?" he asked.

Frankie couldn't think of an answer. This was bad. Really bad.

Max nudged him with his nose. "Come on, fellas," he said. "We can still win. It's just like Louise has been red-carded and ejected. We'll play on."

Frankie shook his head. "Louise has never even been given a *yellow* card before. She's the fairest player I know."

"Maybe we can break her out!" said Charlie, his face brightening. "Isn't that what they do in the movies, Max?"

Frankie's dog whined. "Normally they use dynamite. I'm guessing you don't have any hanging around?"

Charlie buried his head again.

Frankie eyed the clock. Not much time before the game. What if they lost? *If we don't win, we might never get home. . . .*

The sound of pounding hooves interrupted his thoughts. Across the street, they saw the candy-store owner scurry indoors. More shutters banged closed.

In a cloud of dust, three horses galloped into town.

"It looks like the Cowboy's Crew is here," said Frankie.

CHAPTER 4

The lead horse was a brown stallion, ridden by a tall, lean man with a moustache, spinning a lasso over his head. He wore a tight-fitting suit with a black hat and black boots. Thick stubble covered his cheeks, and he chewed what looked like a piece of licorice with his blackened teeth.

His nose had a kink in the middle where it had been broken.

"That must be Tex," Frankie whispered to the others.

A girl with a scarf pulled up over her face rode a smaller horse. Frankie recognized her at once from the "WANTED" poster: Miss Sue-Ann. As her horse skidded to a halt, she tugged down the scarf and gave a nasty smile.

"She looks nothing like Louise!" said Charlie.

The final rider was a chubby man wearing clothes that were much too small. His shirt buttons were popping, and his belly hung over the top of his trousers. His hat was a huge, floppy-brimmed sombrero. He took it off and fanned his sweating pink face. His mouth had melted chocolate smeared around it.

"Looks like they've got only three players, too," said Max.

"'Fraid not, fluffball," said Tex. "Spike, where are ya?"

Sand blew down the empty street, but no one came.

"Spike! Get out here now!" Tex called.

After another minute of waiting, a thin shadow fell on the street from between two buildings. Then out walked the strangest thing Frankie had ever seen. It was a green cactus, six feet tall and covered in sharp spikes. Its eyes were two holes at the top, with a dark slit for a mouth.

"Darn it, Tex," it said. "I was sunbathing out there."

"Meet Spike," said Tex with a grin. "The prickliest customer in the West."

"And the laziest," muttered Miss Sue-Ann.

The cactus waved a spiky arm at her, and she backed away on her horse. "Quiet, little lady," he said, "or you'll have more holes than a honeycomb."

Frankie stepped forward and

dropped the ball to the ground. "We're not scared of you," he said. "Let's play."

At that very moment, a loud hooting sound filled the air. Everybody turned toward it. In the distance, Frankie saw a cloud of smoke spouting into the sky.

"Looks like the express is early," said the short man on Tex's team.

Tex's eyes narrowed and glinted. "Change of plans, then," he said. "We won't be playing soccer today, team."

"Aw, why not?" asked Spike the cactus. "I was looking forward to beating these critters."

"Because we got a train to rob!" said Tex.

Frankie shot Charlie a glance. "This isn't right," he said.

"It's none of our business," said Charlie.

"We can't let them rob the train," said Max. "A real cowboy would stop them."

"You're not a real cowboy," said Charlie. "You're just a . . ."

Frankie left them arguing and rushed to the door of the sheriff's office. He banged on it with his fist until the sheriff opened up. The old man's face looked angry. "I told you before, unless you want to join your friend here —"

"Sheriff, the Cowboy's Crew is here and they're going to rob the express train," said Frankie.

The sheriff's eyes widened, then he pushed past Frankie and shuffled out into the street.

"Hold it right there, Tex," he shouted. "You're going to jail!"

A lasso fell over the sheriff's shoulders. Tex laughed and gave it a tug, pulling him off his feet. Sheriff Quigley struggled, but the rope was too tight. "Why, you varmint!" he yelled. "Let me go this instant. When

Deputy Sandy gets into town, you'll pay for this."

"Oh, is that right?" said Tex. "What do you say, Sandy?"

The chubby man rode up on his horse. "Sorry, Sheriff," he said, stuffing another chocolate bar into his mouth. "I'm with Tex now."

The sheriff goggled. "But, Sandy, you're a *sworn* deputy!"

Sandy pulled something out of his pocket and threw it to the ground, along with the chocolate wrapper. Frankie saw that it was a badge. "Not anymore," he said. "Being an outlaw's much more fun."

Frankie ran forward and started to loosen the rope around the sheriff, and Max joined him. He heard a click and turned to see Tex pointing the barrel of a pistol right at him. "Enough," said the villain. "This thing's loaded with chewing gum. All of you are going to spend some time behind bars."

Max growled as Miss Sue-Ann took the sheriff's gun and pointed it at him. "Don't fight," said Frankie. "Remember how long it takes to get chewing gum out of your fur."

"Inside," said Tex, nodding to the jailhouse. Spike approached menacingly. Frankie didn't want to get anywhere near those spikes. "Come on, guys," he said. "We don't have a choice."

All three were pushed into the jailhouse with the sheriff.

Louise saw them from her cell. She ran to the bars. "What's going on?" she said.

"We got you some company is what," said Sandy.

He unlocked the cage and shoved Frankie, his friends, and the sheriff inside. The door clanged shut again. Sandy hung the keys on a peg on the wall. "Someone might come for you in a few days," he said. "See ya, Sheriff."

He walked out, chuckling to himself.

"What now?" asked Charlie.

Frankie grabbed the bars and tried to bend them. He strained until he thought his bones would break, but the bars didn't budge. Charlie tried, too, and Louise. They all fell back, panting.

"You're wasting your time," sighed the sheriff, shaking free Tex's rope from his shoulders. "They're solid

iron. Better just relax and wait this one out." He sat on the floor and tugged his hat over his eyes.

"We need to beat Tex," said Louise. "Otherwise we're stuck here."

"Maybe Max can squeeze through the bars," said Charlie.

The little dog cocked his head. "It'll be a tight squeeze."

"Just try," said Charlie.

Max pushed his head between the bars, and wriggled. He got about halfway, but no farther. "It's too narrow," he whined, scrambling loose and back into the cell.

"Too many doggy treats, you mean," said Charlie.

The group fell silent. "What's on that train, anyway?" asked Frankie.

The sheriff spoke from beneath his hat. "The biggest shipment of sweets you've ever seen," he said. "If Tex steals them, the kids in all the towns around won't have sweets for a year."

"What a nightmare!" said Charlie.

Frankie stared at the keys hanging on the peg. *There's got to be some way of reaching them.* He kicked the soccer ball against the wall in frustration. As it bounced back, an idea hit him.

"Guys," he said. "I think I might have a plan. Give me your shoelaces."

"How's that gonna help?" asked Sheriff Quigley.

"Just do it," said Louise. Soon Frankie had four laces, all a couple of feet long. He tied them together and wrapped one end around the old soccer ball.

"I get it!" said Louise.

"I don't," said Max.

Frankie pushed the ball between the bars. It was just deflated enough to fit. Then, holding one end of the laces in his left hand, he threw the ball toward the peg. It bounced off the wall right next to them.

"Smart!" said Charlie. "Try again."

On the second attempt, Frankie

knocked the keys off the peg and they clattered to the floor. He threw the ball again and it landed on top of them. Tugging the laces, the ball dragged the keys toward him. In no time at all, he had them in his hands.

"Good thinking, kid," said the sheriff.

Frankie turned the key in the lock and the door *thunked* open. He turned to the others with a grim smile. "Time to stop the Cowboy's Crew," he said.

CHAPTER 5

They peered out from the jailhouse. The street was quiet. Tex had tied his gang's horses to a hitching post in front of the station house. The train had pulled into the station. "This is silly," said the sheriff. "They've got weapons! I bet chewing gum bullets really bruise!"

"We've got *this*," said Frankie, holding up the sagging magic soccer ball.

"And *this*," said Louise, retrieving the lasso rope from the cell.

"And these," said Charlie, waving his goalie gloves.

Everyone looked at Max. "I've got my cowboy know-how," he said. "And sharp teeth."

"You don't have to come," said Frankie to the sheriff. "This is our problem."

Sheriff Quigley grinned. "Good idea. I'll hold the fort here."

Frankie rolled his eyes and walked out. They crept across the dusty street silently and walked up alongside the station house. Frankie paused at the corner of the building and edged his head around. The stationmaster was standing with his arms above his head while Sandy unloaded crates from a train car. Spike was basking in the sun with his arms out.

"Hey, porcupine!" said Tex. "Don't go setting down roots there. Help Sandy."

Grumbling, Spike shuffled over and stabbed a crate with his arms, hoisting it off the train.

Soon they had a dozen crates on the platform.

"Check them," said Tex.

Sandy took a crowbar and inserted it under one of the crate's lids. He levered it off with a crack, and a grin spread over his face.

"It's gold, boss!" he said. "Pure gold."

He lifted a gold nugget the size of an egg out of the crate and held it up to the light. Frankie frowned. *I thought it was sweets they were after.*

"Let me see," said Miss Sue-Ann.

Sandy tossed the nugget to her, and she unwrapped it. She threw the gold wrapper on the platform, and bit into what was inside.

"It's chocolate!" whispered Charlie over Frankie's shoulder.

"Stop drooling," said Max.

"Right," said Frankie. "We need to work as a team. If we all rush at them together, they won't have time to draw their gum guns."

"Like a defense with too many forwards to guard," said Louise.

"I'll handle Tex," said Frankie. "Ready?"

Charlie nodded. "I'm always ready."

"Sure thing, partner," growled Max.

Frankie put his fingers to his lips and let out a whistle. All of Tex's gang looked up. Frankie dropped the ball and volleyed it at Tex. It struck his hand and sent the gun spinning into the air. Charlie ran forward, dove, and caught it. Miss Sue-Ann went for her gun, but the lasso dropped over her shoulders, pinning her arms.

Sandy was too quick. He leapt over a crate as Max dashed at him, and whipped his pistol out of its holster. He cowered behind Spike. "No one move!" he said, aiming it at Frankie. "This is loaded with jawbreakers, and they sure hurt."

Charlie had his gun leveled at Tex. Miss Sue-Ann squirmed in the rope.

Tex smiled, showing off his blackened teeth. "Looks like we've got ourselves a standoff," he said.

"It's almost noon," said Frankie. "How about we settle this the old-fashioned way—a game of soccer?"

Tex stared hard at Frankie, and Frankie held his gaze.

Then the cowboy nodded. "Sure thing. Put the weapon down, Sandy. We're going to school these children some hard lessons."

The two teams lined up at opposite ends of the street. The town had come alive at last. Shutters and doors were flung open as the people of Sweetsville emerged from hiding. Frankie heard two old women muttering to each other under a parasol: "Three young'uns and a dog. They ain't got a chocolate's chance under a blazing sun!"

"And why's that boy wearing gloves? It must be eighty degrees in the shade."

Charlie must have heard. "The best goalies are always . . . never mind." He brushed a lock of damp hair off his head.

Frankie let himself smile. Charlie would need to be *extra* ready if they were going to win today.

The teams had moved two wagons to act as goals. Charlie stood in front of theirs, and Spike the cactus was opposite, flexing his long green limbs. His spines glistened in the sunlight, deadly sharp.

The stationmaster stood in the center with the ball. "We play until the clock strikes twelve," he said. "The winner can take the train out of town; the losers are going to jail for a long, long time."

The crowd stopped chattering and silence fell over the street. Frankie eyed the clock: eleven fifty-seven. Only three minutes to go. He looked across at Louise. She wore a determined face. And Max stood ready to pounce. *We can do it*, thought Frankie.

The stationmaster blew a whistle and Frankie ran for the ball. He got there before Tex and avoided a sliding tackle. Deputy Sandy tried to barge into him, but Frankie managed to skip past and stay on his feet.

"Pass it!" he heard Louise shout, but when Frankie looked he saw Miss Sue-Ann was guarding her closely. Frankie sprinted toward the goal. Spike watched him with beady eyes, spreading his limbs wide. *This is my chance*, thought Frankie. He aimed at the bottom corner and fired.

Spike shot out a leg, and the ball hit one of his spikes. It stuck fast, rather than bouncing off. Frankie kicked the dirt in disgust.

Spike shook his leg, but couldn't get the ball off.

"Hurry up!" said Tex.

Spike managed to knock the ball from his leg, but it stuck to his arm instead. "Just a minute!" he muttered, thrashing his limb.

Max chuckled.

"Ball hogger!" muttered Miss Sue-Ann.

The cactus goalie finally managed to hurl the ball out to Sandy, already red-faced from running around. Frankie couldn't see Tex anywhere. Max scampered up to tackle the deputy, but as he got close, a horse came charging onto the field. A quick glance and Frankie saw why — Tex was by the hitching post. *He must have untied it!*

The horse stampeded in front of Max, who just avoided being

trampled. It gave Sandy time to pass the ball to Miss Sue-Ann. Quick as a whirlwind, she spun away from Louise and angled a shot at goal. She kicked up a load of dust, too. Charlie had to cover his eyes to protect them, and the ball sailed into the back of the open wagon.

Tex punched the air. "That's more like it!" He looked down his broken nose at Frankie. "You won't be getting any candy in jail, scamp. One–nothing to the Crew!"

CHAPTER 6

Charlie fished the ball out of the back of the wagon, looking glum. Frankie eyed the clock. Just over one minute left.

"Keep your heads up, team," said Frankie. "You know what Mr. Donald says: 'Play until the final whistle.'"

Charlie rolled the ball out to Frankie. He saw Sandy barreling toward him, sweat pouring from under his hat. His gait was so wide from riding horses, Frankie had no problem toeing the ball between his legs. Sandy tried to stop himself but it was too late. He tripped over the edge of a horse trough, and fell headfirst into the water with a splash.

"He needed a bath," said one of the spectators.

"You fool!" yelled Tex.

Frankie slid a pass along the ground to Louise. As soon as she had the ball, Miss Sue-Ann rocketed toward her. She was one of the quickest players Frankie had ever seen. Louise glanced up. Max scampered along the wing, but Tex was blocking the pass.

She's got no options! thought Frankie.

Then he saw one.

"Look up, Louise!" he cried.

Louise glanced upward. Frankie knew how quickly her brain worked on the field.

She stabbed the ball high into the air with her left foot, away from everyone. The spectators groaned, thinking she'd mishit it. But the ball crashed right into the "General

Store" sign over the shop and bounced back onto the field. Right by Max's paws.

"Great pass, Louise!" shouted Charlie.

I knew she could do it! thought Frankie.

Max kept the ball close to his feet as he ran toward the goal. Tex charged up behind him, and Spike edged forward, swinging his deadly arms. Frankie chanced a look at the clock. The hands were nearly vertical. Seconds until noon.

"Shoot, Max!" he said.

Max's paws were a blur of step overs and dummies, his tongue lolling. Tex was almost on him. Spike narrowed the angles ahead.

"Shoot now!" cried Louise.

Frankie could hardly watch. The ball bobbled in front of Max, and the little dog thrust his head onto it. Spike wasn't ready for a header and flailed with his arm. The ball sailed over the top, and landed with a thump in the wagon's mouth.

Max rolled sideways as Tex tried to skid to a halt. But his momentum was too fast. Tex crashed into Spike and they fell over together.

"Ouch!" Tex cried. "Ooh! Get off me! Argh! Ouch!"

Frankie winced as he watched Tex

jerk and writhe to free himself of the spikes.

Louise was on her knees, tickling Max's stomach as he rolled over in celebration.

GONG! The clock struck noon.

"One–up! We're tied!" shouted Charlie, clapping his gloves together.

Tex finally untangled himself, his suit torn to ribbons and red scratches covering his skin. He looked very angry indeed.

"There's only one way to decide the winner," he snapped, his eyes glinting as he pointed at Frankie. "A shoot–out between captains."

"No way," said Louise. "Frankie's not a gunslinger."

"Not my problem," said Tex. "We stand back to back, take ten paces, then turn and fire."

"You'd better be quick," said the stationmaster. "The train goes any minute, and the next one's not for a month."

"I don't want to stay here a month," said Charlie. "There aren't any sweets!"

Frankie swallowed. "How about I use the ball instead of a gun?" he asked.

Tex shrugged. "You can use whatever you want," he said, "but nothing travels as quick as a gum bullet."

"I'll do it," said Frankie.

Louise rushed up to him. "Frankie, don't," she said. "It's too dangerous."

"There's no other way," he said. "Just stand back, Louise."

He turned and stood with his back to Tex's, the ball at his feet. The stationmaster hovered beside them. "I'll count to ten," he said. "You both ready?"

"I'm ready to show this young'un who's boss," said Tex.

"I'm ready," said Frankie. But already he was worried. If he kicked the ball at Tex, he might hurt him.

And what was to stop a crook like that just shooting him anyway?

"Right . . . one!" began the station-master. Frankie took a step, and a plan formed in his mind.

"Two . . . three . . . four . . ."

Frankie's heart was thumping. He tried to clear his head. He felt like he was back facing St. Peter's, running toward the goal. *You know what you need to do,* he thought.

"Five . . . six . . . seven . . ."

Aim in your mind. See the target . . .

"Eight . . . nine . . ."

Just focus . . . breathe in . . .

"Ten!"

Frankie spun around and saw Tex's hand reaching lightning fast for his gun. He snapped his foot around, almost by instinct, and blasted the ball just as Tex leveled his six-shooter.

The ball slammed into Tex's hand, and the cowboy's gun went off. Chewing gum whistled past Frankie's

ear. Tex, arms flailing, staggered backward, tripping over his own feet. He landed with a splat on his backside. The crowd gasped and Frankie realized why.

Tex was sitting in a pile of cactus spikes. "What? Ugh!" He tried to stand, but slipped over, sticking himself more. The people of Sweetsville started to laugh.

"It's not funny!" said Tex, as he finally managed to stand. "Stop laughing!"

The spectators were doubled over, slapping one another on the back.

Tex's face blackened with rage. He looked to his gang. "Enough!

I'm not losing to a bunch of kids! Seize them!"

But his gang didn't move.

"Spike, what are you waiting for?"

The cactus man shrugged his spiny shoulders. "They won fair and square, Tex."

"Sue-Ann, don't just stand there!" said Tex.

Miss Sue-Ann shook her head. "It's over, Tex."

"Call yourself an outlaw?" he said.

Miss Sue-Ann threw her gun to the ground. "Actually, I wouldn't mind just working for a living. Maybe I'll get a job in the candy store."

Tex stamped his foot. "Sandy, tie them up!"

But Sandy edged away. "I'm done, Tex," he said. He turned to Sheriff Quigley. "Would you have me back, Boss? I'll work double shifts."

The sheriff thought for a long moment, then nodded. He pointed to Tex. "You can start by putting *him* behind bars."

The people of Sweetsville broke into applause as Sandy and the sheriff gripped Tex by the shoulders.

He writhed but couldn't get loose. "Let go of me, you wretches!" The crowd parted as he was dragged toward the jailhouse. "You haven't heard the last of Tex!"

Frankie, laughing, felt a glove tapping him on the shoulder. It was Charlie, and he didn't look happy.

"I think we'd better get going," said his friend.

Frankie peered over his shoulder. Sure enough, two jets of steam spouted from the train.

Slowly, it started to move.

CHAPTER 7

"Time to say good-bye!" yelled Frankie, snatching up his soccer ball. "Come on, guys!"

With Louise, Charlie, and Max, he sprinted toward the train station building. The crowd cheered as they passed and the stationmaster raised his hand to wave. "See you again soon," he said, with a twinkle in his eye.

Frankie burst onto the platform and leapt over a crate of sweets. The train was picking up speed, tooting as it pulled out of the station. Frankie spotted a door and ran alongside. Louise got a foot on the step and hauled herself onboard. Frankie let Charlie go next. His thighs were pumping just to keep up.

"Wait for me!" barked Max. "I've got short legs!"

Frankie saw Max darting along as fast as he could, but the train was quicker. Frankie hurled the ball to

Louise and bent down to scoop the dog up in his arms. He dashed after the train. But carrying Max slowed him down. *I can't keep this up for much longer . . .*

"Charlie! I'm going to have to throw Max to you!" he yelled.

"Huh?" said Max. "We didn't discuss this."

"You ready?" said Frankie.

"No!" said Max.

"I'm always ready!" said Charlie, holding out his gloves.

Frankie saw the end of the platform approaching fast. *I don't have much time.* Taking aim, he hurled Max toward the door.

Charlie snatched him from the air and bundled him inside.

Frankie's legs burned and his heart pounded so hard he felt it might burst out of his chest. The train wheels chugged in a blur and smoke drifted from the engine.

I'm not going to make it. . . .

"Come on, Frankie!" Louise shouted. "Don't give up."

Louise's words fired Frankie's spirit. He gritted his teeth and forced an extra burst of speed, throwing himself at the door. His fingers caught the edge and the train dragged him off his feet. Then he felt hands gripping his arms and yanking him onboard. He landed in a heap on top of Louise and Charlie.

"Thanks, guys," he said.

Once he found his footing again, he stuck his head out of the train door. Wind whistled past as the town of Sweetsville faded into the distance.

"Um . . . what now?" asked Louise. "Do you think this train will take us home?"

"Who cares?" said Charlie. "Look what I found." He pulled the lid off a box and scooped out a handful of candy. "Jelly beans!"

The train thundered on through the desert. Frankie scanned the horizon but couldn't see any sign of life or any landmarks. Then, ahead, he spied a tunnel where the tracks plunged into a mountainside. He wondered what was on the other side.

"These are delicious!" said Charlie. "Do you guys want —"

The train reached the tunnel and darkness swallowed them. The carriage beneath Frankie's feet seemed to disappear. For a moment, he felt completely weightless, as if he were floating. Then he rolled over and over on the ground. He heard the others crying out. Max barked and several horses whinnied and snorted.

Frankie sat up and picked a piece of straw from his hair. Max was licking his face. As his eyes adjusted to the gloom, he realized where he was.

"The stable!" he gasped. "We're home."

Charlie shook the straw off his clothes and opened one glove. In it was a single jelly bean.

"Sorry, guys, only one left," he said, and popped it into his mouth.

The following week, Frankie and his team were up against Ryle's Park Elementary School.

Louise ran down the wing past two players, then squared the ball sideways to Frankie. Just as he was about to shoot, a defender clipped his ankle and Frankie sprawled on the grass.

The ref blew his whistle and pointed to the penalty spot.

Frankie picked himself up, grabbed the ball, and placed it on the penalty spot. Mr. Donald was standing behind the goal. "It's okay if you don't want to take it, Frankie," he said. "You know — after last week's miss? No one would blame you if you wanted Louise to go instead."

Frankie glanced at Louise. She smiled. "You take it, Frankie. We all believe in you."

Kevin was sulking on the sidelines with Frankie's parents. As Frankie took a few steps back, he heard his brother mutter, "The loser returns."

Frankie let the words sink away and focused on the ball. If he could beat Tex the outlaw in a shoot-out, scoring a penalty against Ryle's Park Elementary was nothing.

Just believe in yourself.

Frankie took three steps and swung his cleat. It connected perfectly and drove the ball into the top of the goal. The net ballooned and Frankie's team cheered.

Frankie slid across the grass on his knees, lifted his hands to the sky, and shouted:

"YEE–HAW!"

ACKNOWLEDGMENTS

Many thanks to everyone at Little, Brown Book Group UK; Neil Blair, Zoe King, Daniel Teweles, and all at The Blair Partnership; Mike Jackson for bringing my characters to life; special thanks to Michael Ford for all his wisdom and patience; and to Steve Kutner for being a great friend and for all his help and guidance not just with this book but with everything.

DON'T MISS FRANKIE'S OTHER ADVENTURES!

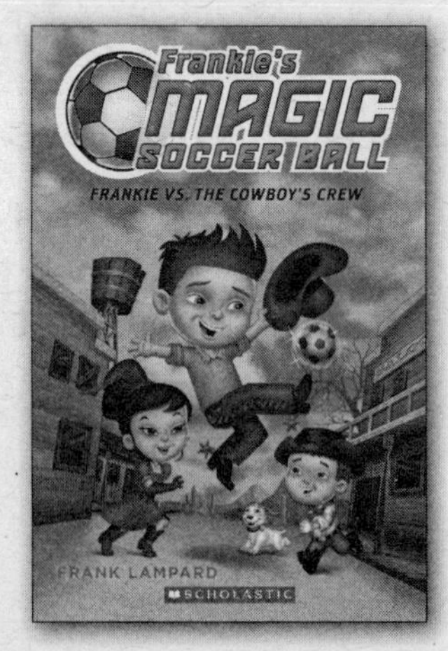